WALT DISNEY'S

The
Brave Little Tailor

Random House New York

Library of Congress Cataloging in Publication Data
Walt Disney's The brave little tailor. (Disney's wonderful
world of reading, no. 18). When Mickey the tailor kills seven
flies, everyone thinks they were seven giants and he inad-
vertently becomes the king's giant-killer. [1. Fairy tales]
I. Title: The brave little tailor. PZ8.W1917 [398.2] [E]
74-1253 ISBN 0-394-82559-4 ISBN 0-394-92559-9 (lib. bdg.)
Manufactured in the United States of America
F G H I J K
9

Once there was a town in terrible trouble.

A huge giant lived nearby.

Every time the giant sat down on a house, he crushed it.

Everyone was afraid the giant would crush the whole town.

Everyone, that is, but Mickey the tailor.
He had a different kind of trouble.
Some flies had gotten into his house.
They were buzzing all around his head.

At last Mickey grabbed
his fly swatter.

He slammed it down
on the table.

He picked it up and counted seven dead flies.
"Wow!" he said. "Seven with one blow!
I must tell someone about this."

Two farmers were talking near Mickey's shop.

"We must get rid of the giant," said one.

"But who can do it?" asked the other.

Just then Mickey opened his window and cried:

"I killed seven with one blow!"

The farmers thought Mickey was talking
about giants, not flies.

They ran and told everyone.

"The tailor killed seven giants
with one blow," they said.

One farmer
even told
the king's
baker.

The baker ran off
to tell the king's knight.

"Did you hear?" said the baker.
"The tailor killed seven giants with
one blow!"

"The little tailor is braver
than he looks!" said the knight.
"The king must hear about this."
And off he ran to tell the king.

As soon as the king heard the news,
he sent for the little tailor.

Mickey smiled at the king
and the beautiful Princess Minnie.

"Gee," thought Mickey. "Maybe the king
wants me to make him a new coat."

"Little tailor," said the king, "tell me how
you killed seven with one blow."

"Well," said Mickey.
"It was really nothing.

"First they came at me
from the right.

"Then they came at me
from the left.

"Suddenly they were
all around me.

"So I let them
have it.

"They never knew
what hit them."

"Bravo!" cried the king.

"You shall be my giant-killer."

"GIANT-killer? ? ?" said Mickey.

"I could never be your giant-killer."

"I will give you gold," said the king.

"No thanks," said Mickey.

"Gold will not make me change my mind."

Just then Princess Minnie whispered something in the king's ear.

"Of course!" said the king.

"Little tailor," said the king,
"if you will be my giant-killer
you may marry the princess."
Mickey looked at Minnie.
"Golly, gee whillikers!" he said.

So the little tailor became
the king's giant-killer.
   And off he went
to find the giant.

As soon as Mickey was alone
he sat down to think.

"I am just a tailor," he thought.
"What do I know about killing giants?"

Mickey was thinking so hard, he did not
see the dark shadow on the ground.

When he did look up, he saw a huge foot.
It was the giant about to step on him!
But Mickey was fast.

He ran to the first thing he saw—
a wagon full of pumpkins.
He jumped inside and hid.

Mickey heard a loud CRUNCH.
He peeked out.
The giant was sitting on a house.
The house was crushed to the ground.
But the giant just looked at the pumpkins.
"Ah, some orange berries!" he said.

The giant reached down and grabbed a bunch
of pumpkins.

Without knowing it, he grabbed Mickey, too.

The giant opened his mouth
and popped in the pumpkins.
But Mickey was fast.
He grabbed the first thing he saw —
the giant's mustache.

Mickey was hanging by a hair.

The giant felt something tickle him under his nose.

"Darn fly!" said the giant.

And he caught Mickey
between his fingers.

"Now is the time
to be brave," said Mickey.
He took out his scissors.
"On guard!" he cried.

And he poked the giant in the nose.

"Ouch!" said the giant.
And he slammed his hands together.
But Mickey was fast.
He jumped into the first thing he saw —
the giant's sleeve.

Now the giant felt something tickle his arm.
So he reached into his sleeve to get it.
But again Mickey was too fast for the giant.
He cut his way out of the sleeve
with his scissors.

Then Mickey took out his needle and thread.

He began to sew very fast.

First he sewed around the giant's fingers.

Then he sewed the giant's sleeves together.

Next he wrapped the thread
around the giant's nose.

But he didn't stop there.

Around and around
went Mickey.

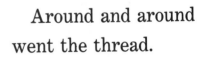

Around and around
went the thread.

At last the giant was all sewn up.
He could not move.
He could not even stand up.

The giant fell down with a great crash!

Everyone in town heard the crash.
They ran to see what it was.
There was Mickey standing on the giant's foot.
"Three cheers for the brave little tailor!"
they cried.

They carried Mickey
back to the castle.
Minnie was waiting
at the gate.

Soon the brave little tailor
and the beautiful Princess Minnie
were happily married.
And to think it all began
with seven dead flies.